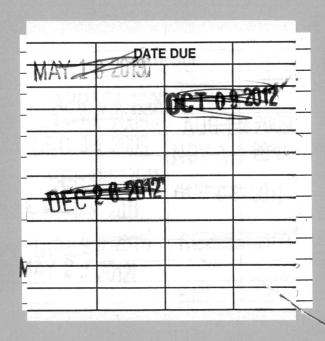

Full Color

Etienne Delessert

CREATIVE EDITIONS

MANKATO, MINNESOTA

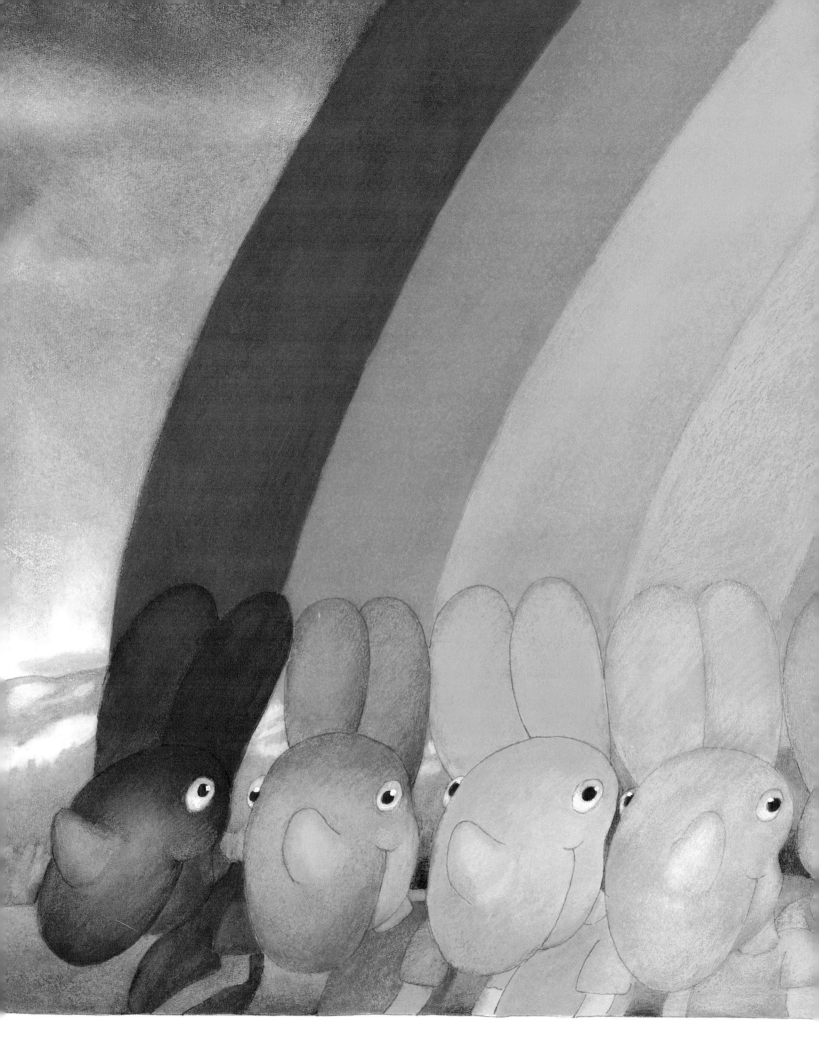

Sometimes we see a rainbow after a storm.

A rainbow is made of seven colors.

orange

like flames

yellow
like the sun

green

like grass

blue

like water

indigo

like dye

violet

like a tulip

three primary colors
mixing them creates all
of nature's colors

red and yellow
become orange

blue and yellow

become green

red and blue
become purple

red and yellow
become orange

red, blue, and yellow
become brown

white
a white surface
reflects all colors

black
a black surface
absorbs all colors

Beautiful colors
are made by mixing tints
of many colors

Text and illustrations copyright © 2008 Etienne Delessert

Published in 2008 by Creative Editions

P.O. Box 227, Mankato, MN 56002 USA

Creative Editions is an imprint of The Creative Company.

First published in 2005 by Gallimard Jeunesse,

Tout en couleur, as part of an anthology entitled *Jeux d'enfant.*

Designed by Rita Marshall

Printed in Italy

Library of Congress Cataloging-in-Publication Data

Delessert, Etienne.

Full color / by Etienne Delessert.

ISBN 978-1-56846-206-6

1. Colors—Juvenile literature. I. Title.

QC495.5.D43 2008

535.6—dc22   2007040406

First edition

2 4 6 8 9 7 5 3 1